nickelodeon
HOUSE OF
ANUBIS

The Eye of Horus

Adapted by Peter McGrath

Based on the script by Hans Bourlon,
Gert Verhulst, and Anjali Taneja

Random House New York

"**W**ow!" exclaimed Nina Martin. She gazed, awestruck, at a redbrick Victorian house overgrown with ivy and crumbling with age. She took a deep breath and climbed the front steps of the ancient building.

Nina had won a scholarship to England's top boarding school but had arrived two weeks after the term had started. She had been given directions to Anubis House, where she would live with seven other students until the end of the school year. She hoped there was still time to make friends.

Nina reached the top step and stopped in front of a large wooden door. Before she could knock, it swung open silently.

No one was behind the door.

Nina shivered. Had there been a strong gust of

1

wind? She entered the foyer and looked around. On her left was a spiral staircase winding up to the second floor. The woodwork formed curious eye shapes between the balusters. Propped up on the side of the staircase was an Egyptian casket that looked like it belonged in a museum. Pale yellow light from small lamps reflected off the black-and-red tiled floor.

As Nina peered into the next room, the front door slammed shut. She glanced behind her. There was still no one at the door.

Nina turned around and gasped. A tall man with cold, dark eyes scowled down at her.

"Isn't the bell working?" he said, moving closer.

"No . . . well, um . . . yes. I don't know. The door w-was open," stammered Nina.

"And so you just walked right in?" the man barked.

"Well, that's how we normally deal with doors in America," Nina replied pluckily.

"You're late!" said the man. "Two weeks late!"

"I know," replied Nina, "but my scholarship was delayed, and then my Gran got sick, and—"

"I am not inclined to listen to your life story. Now, here are the rules. . . ."

At that moment, a cheery and pleasant-mannered lady bounded down the stairs. She had dark hair and a twinkle in her eye.

"Victor Emmanuel Rodenmaar, I hope you are giving the new girl our warmest welcome!" Turning to Nina, the bundle of energy announced herself as Trudy Rehman.

"I am your house mother. Welcome to Anubis House. It's a little spooky, and Victor can be difficult. But it's the best place on campus." Trudy smiled warmly, and Nina began to feel a little more at home.

Victor frowned and clasped the front of his jacket, preparing to give Nina the history of the house. "The Anubis estate was built in 1890, although it wasn't actually named Anubis until 1922."

Trudy giggled. "Nina doesn't care about all that boringness, Victor! She's a teenager!" She took Nina's arm and led her into a living room filled with dark leather couches and a wooden coffee table. Tall windows framed by red velvet curtains let in the afternoon light, which faded into the darkness of the large fireplace.

Nina looked around in awe. "Everything is so old and beautiful! This house must have a ton of stories."

Trudy smiled. She pointed to the next room, which held a large table with eight chairs gathered around it. "Now, this is where I serve breakfast and evening meals—delicious!" she declared. Beyond the dining room lay the kitchen.

As Nina looked at the walls of the dining room, she spotted an old portrait of a man and a woman. She sensed something mysterious and sad about them.

Victor came up behind her. "That's Mr. and Mrs. Frobisher-Smythe, the original occupants of the house." He shook his head. "They died—tragically."

Before Nina could ask how the Frobisher-Smythes had died, Victor led her and Trudy back into the foyer. As they climbed the stairs, he sternly explained the rules. "The boys' rooms are downstairs. We don't want anyone wandering around after nine o'clock, and all lights must be out by ten." At the top of the stairs, Victor pointed to an office. Nina peered through the glass—on top of the desk sat a creepy-looking stuffed raven. A cabinet with spare keys hung from the wall. "This is my office, and needless to say, it is strictly off-limits," Victor said.

Past Victor's office was a hallway that led to the

girls' rooms. Nina pointed to a narrow wooden door that seemed out of place. "What's that?" she asked Trudy.

"That's the door to the attic," Trudy replied.

Victor spoke grimly. "Going up into the attic or down into the cellar is strictly forbidden. Is that understood?"

"Crystal clear," replied Nina.

Victor opened another door. "This is your room."

Nina found herself in a purple room with two twin beds. One wall was covered with black-and-white Gothic posters, and clothes lay scattered about. The other side was almost bare. There were no decorations except for a photograph of two smiling girls, taped to a wardrobe door.

Nina peered at the photograph. "Who are they?" she asked.

"Oh, that's Joy's—" began Trudy.

"Joy. Has. Left," Victor said, ripping the photo off the wardrobe and crumpling it in his hand.

"Very suddenly and unexpectedly, if I may say so," said Trudy.

Victor glowered at her. "You may not." He turned to Nina and gestured toward the floor. "Your suitcases have arrived. I will leave you to unpack." He strode icily out of the room.

Nina was just settling in when a slim girl with blue and purple extensions streaking her dark hair rushed in, red-faced and very angry. Nina recognized her from the photograph Victor had destroyed.

"Where's Joy?" the girl demanded. "What have you done with my best friend?"

"I don't know Joy. I've just arrived from America," Nina said, baffled.

"You've stolen her phone!" the girl yelled, snatching Joy's phone from her former bed. "Get out! You're not my roommate—Joy is!" She grabbed Nina roughly and threw her out of the room. Nina ducked out of the way as the girl threw her blankets and suitcases into the hallway.

"But I don't know where Joy is," said Nina, on the verge of tears. "Her stuff was gone when I got here."

Just then, Victor arrived. "Patricia Williamson, what is going on?" he thundered.

Patricia tossed back a lock of blue hair. "Where's Joy?" she bellowed back.

Victor explained that Joy's parents had arrived at the school and removed her earlier that day.

Patricia crossed her arms. "Why would they do that?"

"I have absolutely no idea," Victor said impatiently.

Patricia's eyes narrowed. "I don't believe you! Joy would never leave without saying goodbye. Or without her phone and her Bunzibuns," she said, picking up a stuffed rabbit from Joy's bed. "Bunzibuns is her favorite cuddly toy."

Victor motioned to Joy's phone and stuffed rabbit. "Give them to me and I'll forward them along."

Patricia reluctantly handed over Joy's beloved possessions. She glared at Victor. "I'll get to the bottom of this!" she shouted, and stormed downstairs.

Victor shoved Nina's blankets into her arms. "Dinner will be ready in ten minutes," he said, leaving her to clean up the mess Patricia had made.

2

While Nina put away her belongings, six other Anubis House students gathered in the living room downstairs. Patricia had told the group about Joy's disappearance. "I can't believe nobody's got her home phone number," she groaned.

A girl with blond hair and wearing an expensive pink dress gestured around the room. "That's because this *is* her home. Just call her cell phone."

Patricia sighed. "Amber, keep up. I told you—she left her phone behind."

Amber rolled her blue-gray eyes. "So . . . text her."

"Stupidity leak," Patricia muttered.

"So, Joy's just *gone*?" asked Mara, a shy, dark-haired girl with brown eyes. "That is really weird."

A skinny boy named Alfie got a devious twinkle in his eye. "Maybe Joy has been abducted by aliens—

8

and maybe the new girl is one of them."

Alfie's friend Jerome laughed. "Yeah, maybe the new girl is an alien in a flesh suit."

A hush fell as Nina walked in.

"Hi. I'm Nina," she said nervously. "I'm from America." She looked around the room. The only response came from a dark-haired boy named Fabian.

"Hey!" he said.

Alfie said, "Hello . . . space girl," which made the others laugh. Nina shifted uncomfortably.

"Dinner's ready," called Trudy from the dining room.

The students moved to their places at the table. When Nina tried to sit down, Amber claimed the seat as hers. Patricia grinned at Nina's embarrassment; then her grin faded to a glower. "So, when are you going to tell us what you know about Joy's disappearance, Nina?" she hissed.

"I guess when I actually know something," Nina said.

"Oh, come on!" shouted Patricia, leaping up from her chair. "One minute I'm sitting in class next to Joy, and the next minute I find you in our room, with her phone! That's too much of a coincidence. I don't know what you've done with her, but I intend to find out." Patricia glared at Nina and stalked out. The remaining Anubis House students finished their dinner in silence.

After dinner, Nina went to the living room to read. Patricia attempted to reignite their earlier confrontation, but Nina bit her lip and kept her eyes on her book. Feeling completely alone, she listened to her fellow students carrying on with each other.

Alfie and Jerome were chuckling as they discussed pranks they could pull. Mick, the school's good-looking track star, was struggling through his biology homework, wondering aloud how on earth he would finish it on his own. He had enormous talent on the track but almost none when it came to classes.

Suddenly, Mick jumped up and headed upstairs to Amber and Mara's room. He tapped on their door but didn't wait for an answer before walking in.

Amber was startled. She and Mick had been dating for a short time, but she'd thought he was beginning to lose interest in her. She smiled brightly. "Mick! I just started removing my makeup and I've only got one eye on! But how sweet it is of you to come and see me."

"Actually, it's Mara I've come to see." Mick turned

away from Amber. "I'm struggling with my biology, and as you are the 'biology babe,' I thought maybe you could help me."

In spite of Amber's making serious "Don't you dare!" faces behind Mick's back, Mara agreed. As Mick left, Amber wailed to Mara, "How could you?"

"Don't worry," replied Mara. "He only wants me for my brains. You're drop-dead gorgeous, and he knows it."

"Yes, I am, aren't I?" Amber said smugly. Reassured, she returned to her beauty products and smiled to herself.

At bedtime, the students could hear Victor doing his usual countdown-to-curfew routine, announcing the number of minutes left until lights-out. Victor finished with his trademark routine. "You have five minutes precisely, and then I want to hear a pin drop." As he did every night, he took a pin out of his top left coat pocket and held it high. The pin fell and hit the floor with a small, metallic clink.

Later that night, dark shadows played over Anubis House. In his office, Victor was painting Corbiere, his stuffed raven, a deeper shade of black. When he was done, he locked the door and drew the blinds. He placed Joy's phone on his desk and smashed it to pieces with a hammer. He dropped Bunzibuns and the crumpled picture of Patricia and Joy into a metal trash can next to his desk and lit a match. As he set fire to Joy's belongings, a sinister smile came over his face.

Dear Diary,

What a terrible day! Today I arrived at Anubis House. A really cute guy named Fabian was nice to me, but all the other students were horrible, especially this one girl, Patricia. Just a few minutes ago, I was in the bathroom and used my towel to wipe off a steamy mirror. Patricia and two other students, Amber and Mara, came running in. Patricia told me that "Help me! Joy" had been written on that mirror. Joy was Patricia's best friend, and she disappeared today.

Patricia accused me of erasing Joy's message, but I swear I didn't see anything! I've only been here a few hours, and already I feel like all the other students in the house have turned against me. I hope things become normal soon and that coming to England wasn't a mistake. I feel so lonely. I really miss Gran back home in America.

3

Walking to class the next morning, Patricia came to a decision. "I need to know what happened to Joy!" she thought. She decided to ask Mr. Sweet, the school principal, for help. Mr. Sweet had an annoying habit of quoting Latin to anyone who would listen, but he also had a reputation for being honest. Patricia confronted Mr. Sweet in his office and fired a barrage of questions at the startled man. She insisted that Joy would not have left without telling her, would not have forgotten her phone or Bunzibuns, and certainly would have called her by now if nothing was wrong.

Mr. Sweet looked quite shaken and lost his usual reserved manner. He suggested that maybe Joy did not want to make contact with Patricia.

"*Tempus fugit* . . . time marches on, you know."

"That's not possible," wailed Patricia. "Joy would

have called me. Something has happened to her!"

Nina woke up early that morning. "I need to clear my head," she thought. "A walk in the woods might be the first nice thing I've done since arriving here."

As she walked through the gates of Anubis House, she collided with a white-haired lady who wore only a thin nightgown.

"That's my house," said the woman, pointing at the gloomy Anubis House.

"Er . . . I don't think so," replied Nina.

"That's my house," insisted the woman. Her eyes suddenly widened and she exclaimed, "It's you, isn't it! I knew you would come. I'm Sarah."

Nina wrapped her coat around the strange lady and helped her into the house. Trudy met them at the door.

"There's a nursing home down the road. She's probably wandered up from there," suggested Trudy.

Nina offered to walk Sarah back to the home. When they arrived, they were met by a surprised nurse who explained that the old woman, Emily, did not normally wander off.

"That's odd," said Nina. "She told me her name was Sarah. She must be more confused than I thought."

Nina followed the nurse, who led the old woman into her room and settled her into a comfortable chair with a warm blanket. Nina noticed a photograph of Anubis House on the wall. The nurse offered her a cup of tea, and Nina accepted.

As soon as the nurse had gone, the old woman took an eye-shaped locket from around her neck and passed it to Nina.

"This locket will keep you safe," she whispered. "There is a treasure in the house that only you have the power to find and protect. But be careful. There is danger in that house. It is a dark house. A bad house!"

Nina tried to refuse the locket, but the woman insisted. "Take it, Nina!" she said, closing her eyes. "And remember—my name is Sarah."

Nina was shocked. How did the lady know her name?

The woman drifted off to sleep, saying over and over, "Beware the black bird. Beware the black bird."

Nina suddenly realized she would be late for school. She gave the old lady a quick peck on the cheek, slipped the locket around her neck, and rushed to class.

Dear Diary,

Today Patricia found out that Alfie had written the message on the bathroom mirror as a practical joke. She's still convinced that something bad has happened to Joy, though. And she's still as mean as ever!

Tonight I had a terrible dream. I was surrounded by Victor, Corbiere, and Sarah, the woman from the nursing home. Sarah kept saying, "Beware the black bird. Beware the black bird."

All of a sudden, I woke up. Patricia was above me, dropping feathers from a boa onto my face and cackling, "Beware the black bird, beware the black bird." She jumped off my bed and stomped over to her side of the room, complaining that I had woken her up.

I wasn't able to fall back asleep, so I used my cell phone as a flashlight and opened the locket Sarah gave me. In the dim light, I saw a portrait of a beautiful young woman in 1920s clothing. I wonder if it's Sarah?

4

Morning sunlight slanted through the windows of the dining room. Nina walked into breakfast to find Alfie, Jerome, and Patricia cawing and flapping their arms. She ignored them and sat with Fabian, whom she felt she could trust. She confided the events of the previous day to him and said that her dream had really spooked her.

Then Amber breezed in, flicking her long blond hair casually. Her face darkened when Fabian told her that Mick was studying with Mara.

"It's *okay*. I already knew and it's fine," she lied.

"Look out! Green-eyed monster alert," sneered Jerome.

Changing the subject quickly, Amber asked Nina what her parents were like. Nina explained that they had been killed in a car accident, and she had been raised by her grandmother. There was a hush in the room.

"Oh, I'm sorry. That's awful," said Amber, showing genuine sympathy for the first time.

"That's okay. It was a long time ago," replied Nina, thinking that it really only felt like yesterday.

Once the breakfast dishes had been cleared, Amber went up to her room to confront Mara.

"Hello, Amber," her roommate chirped cheerily.

"I don't want you to see Mick anymore," spat Amber. "You're spending all your time studying with him, and I know you fancy him."

"Well, it may surprise you to learn that Mick is not the fastest learner in the world. And I do not fancy him," insisted Mara, although her cheeks flushed slightly as she spoke.

"Why don't you fancy him? What's wrong with him? Everyone else fancies him!" Amber said

"There's nothing wrong with him," said Mara. "He's going out with you, and that would make him off-limits even if I did fancy him, which I don't."

"I don't care," replied Amber, storming out of the

room. Seconds later she returned, more calmly. "You have no idea how hard it is to be one half of an alpha couple."

Mara flashed a sympathetic smile at Amber as she thought, "It's lucky you don't know that Mick wants me to help him with his physics homework as well, or you'd *really* hit the roof!"

Patricia was convinced that Nina had something to do with Joy's disappearance and was determined to make Nina's life as miserable as possible. With the help of the two pranksters, Jerome and Alfie, she came up with a plan. She was going to make Nina participate in a fake initiation ceremony that involved a visit to the forbidden attic. Nina would have to break into Victor's office, steal the spare attic key, open the door, and bring back something from the attic.

"That will spook her," thought Patricia gleefully. If Victor found Nina there, she would get in a lot of trouble.

At school, Patricia pretended to apologize to Nina for her behavior. As Fabian stood in openmouthed disbelief, Patricia, Jerome, and Alfie gathered around to explain what Nina would need to do to be fully accepted as a member of Anubis House.

"I think it's about time we welcomed you in the traditional way," said Patricia with a smirk.

Fabian frowned. "What are you going on about?"

Patricia turned to Alfie. "Alfie, why don't you tell Nina about the initiation ceremony?"

"Every new person who comes through the school has to go through . . ." Alfie scratched his head. "An initiation ceremony."

Before Fabian could say there was no such thing, Nina agreed to participate. "Sounds like fun. What do I have to do?" she asked.

That evening, Nina, Patricia, Jerome, and Alfie crept up to Victor's office to get the spare key to the attic. Just as they were about to go in, Victor discovered them in the hallway and demanded to know what they were doing. Alfie dropped to his knees.

"This floor. It definitely needs a polish," he said, rubbing his hand back and forth over the surface.

"Right, then. You can polish it," Victor sneered,

bringing Alfie with him to the storage closet to find the cleaning materials.

With Victor gone, Nina seized her chance, darting into the office and grabbing the master keys from his drawer. She opened the cupboard that held the spare keys and quickly snatched the one for the attic. She locked the cupboard and returned the master key to the drawer.

"I did it!" Nina thought proudly. But then she bumped into the desk, knocking over Corbiere. With a gasp she reached out and caught the raven just before it hit the ground. Relieved, she turned and looked up. And there stood Victor, stone-faced, looking down on her like a gargoyle. Patricia and Jerome had fled and were nowhere to be seen.

"Nina Martin! What are you doing?" he rumbled.

"Oh, er . . . I was j-just taking a look at your raven," Nina stammered. "I'm kind of . . . er . . . er . . . an amateur taxidermist."

Victor looked at her skeptically. He didn't believe her, but he wasn't sure what she had been up to either. He gave her a stern warning and told her to get out. "And don't let me catch you in my office ever again!" he yelled.

Nina bolted from Victor's office and ran all the way to her room. Her heart was in her throat, but she smiled as she opened her hand to reveal the attic key.

5

Although Nina now had a key to the attic, she had to wait nervously for the next school day to pass before she could complete the initiation ceremony. In the meantime, there was drama afoot for other Anubis House students. In biology, the students had received their graded assignments. Mick had gotten an A-minus. He was delighted and ran over to Mara after class, picking her up and swinging her around. "Thank you, thank you, thank you! I have never seen a grade like this before!" he gushed.

"Mick, you only got an A-minus because of Mara—get over yourself!" fumed Amber. "Right, that's it," she thought. "I know what I'll do . . . I'll make Mick jealous."

Her opportunity arrived almost immediately. The next class was drama, taught by a young new teacher named Jason Winkler, who also taught English and history. Jason chose Amber and Alfie to read a scene from *Romeo and Juliet*. He gave them each a book as they sauntered to the stage.

Amber was born to perform, but Alfie squirmed uncomfortably. He read, "'Shall I hear more or should I speak at this?'"

Amber replied, "''Tis but thy name that is my enemy; thou art' . . . truly the yummiest boy I have ever seen, Romeo!" And with that, she leapt across the stage and planted a kiss on Alfie.

Alfie's eyes glazed over, and he stood looking blissfully into space. The class gasped in unison as Mick sat in shock.

"I don't believe it," he muttered. "Amber has some explaining to do!"

At the stroke of midnight, the Anubis House students sneaked into Nina's room. It was time for her initiation ceremony. Each student held a flashlight under their chin, casting an eerie glow on their face.

"Nina Martin, you are here to prove you are brave

enough to stay at Anubis House," whispered Patricia in her spookiest voice. "Swear on the graves of all your ancestors that you will never, ever tell a living soul about tonight."

"I swear," replied Nina solemnly.

The floors creaked softly as Patricia led the way to the attic.

"Unlock the door," she commanded.

Taking a deep breath, Nina opened the attic door and started up the stairs. Patricia leapt forward and grabbed the key from Nina. She slammed the door shut and locked it, then put the key in her pocket. The other students stared at her in disbelief.

"What are you doing?" cried Amber.

Patricia ignored Amber and shouted to Nina through the locked door, "What do you know about Joy?"

"Nothing, I know nothing! Let me out," begged Nina.

"If you know nothing, you'll have to stay in there," cackled Patricia.

"Let me out!" screamed Nina. She began frantically banging on the door.

Then Victor appeared from nowhere with a flashlight of his own.

"What's going on here?" he bellowed. "What's all this noise, and why are you all out of bed? Were you trying to get into the attic?"

"No, we thought we heard mice," said Patricia sweetly.

"Get to bed!" barked Victor. As the students rushed to their rooms, Victor opened the attic door and slowly crept up the stairs.

As soon as she had heard Victor's voice, Nina had run. She was terrified, but she was thinking calmly. "If Victor finds me up here, I'll be expelled and I'll lose my scholarship." She searched desperately for a hiding place in the dark, cluttered room but couldn't find one.

Victor reached the top of the steps. Nina was sure he would see her and slumped heavily against a wall, awaiting the inevitable. Suddenly, she saw that the locket Sarah had given her was glowing! An eye-shaped symbol in the center of the wall turned fiery red, and the wall revolved 180 degrees, pushing Nina into a secret room on the other side. She landed with a crash.

Victor heard the loud noise. He shone his flashlight wildly and spotted a rat scurrying along some boxes. "Rodents!" he hissed, and headed back down the stairs.

Nina breathed a sigh of relief, though she was still trapped. "The locket might help me get out," she thought, and placed it next to an eye-shaped symbol on the secret side of the wall. The wall started to turn again. Just before Nina dived to the regular side of the attic, she thought she glimpsed the face of a young woman staring at her from the secret room.

Dear Diary,

Today I nearly got expelled. Patricia locked me in the attic and wouldn't let me out! Victor was about to find me up there when I crashed through a false wall and landed in a secret room. All I can say is there's more than meets the eye in Anubis House.

I was able to use a bobby pin to unlock the attic door, and I found Fabian and Amber on the other side. They were going to tell Victor everything so he would let me out. Thank goodness that didn't happen!

Amber gave me a hug and Fabian told me I was really brave and totally passed the initiation. He's so geek chic. But Patricia is possibly the meanest person I have ever met.

6

Nina overslept the next morning. She dressed quickly and hurried down to breakfast. As she entered the dining hall, everyone stood and applauded—everyone except Patricia.

When they had finished eating, a blushing Fabian asked if Nina would fancy walking to class with him.

Nina laughed. "Yes, I would *fancy* walking to school with you." She shook her head shyly. "Sorry, this all takes some getting used to, I just think . . ."

She trailed off when Fabian dropped to the ground next to some bushes near the house.

"This a little strange, even for England. I'm halfway through a sentence and you dive into the bushes?" Nina asked, bewildered.

"I've got it," Fabian cried triumphantly as he picked up a key and ran back to her. "Patricia threw the attic key into the bushes last night. This needs to get back to Victor's office as soon as possible," he added.

"Not so fast," said Nina. "I'm going back into the attic. I know it sounds crazy, but I think I saw someone up there. I need to know. What if Joy truly *has* disappeared? And what if she's still here somewhere?"

"You do sound crazy, but if you're going back into the attic, then I'm coming with you, and no arguments," said Fabian.

"Wow, that was forceful," said Nina.

"It was rather, wasn't it?" replied Fabian, blushing.

By midday, Patricia was in a foul mood. She stormed into the girls' bathroom and flung her schoolbag at the wall. It landed with a thud and dislodged a tile. "Oh, great. That's all I need," Patricia said.

Sighing as she surveyed the damage, she discovered a small hole between the tiles. She could see right into Mr. Sweet's office! Mr. Sweet was discussing Joy's disappearance with Mrs. Andrews, a matronly French teacher.

"There was no need to take Joy. The betrayer is long dead," said Mr. Sweet solemnly.

"Victor wanted to proceed with caution," replied Mrs. Andrews. "And for once I agreed with him."

"Patricia is determined to find out what happened to Joy," said Mr. Sweet.

"And we must be equally determined to make sure she never does; there is too much at stake."

Patricia, stepped back, numb with fear. "Who is the betrayer?" she thought. "And what does the betrayer have to do with my best friend?" Patricia had been right all along. Something *had* happened to Joy!

Mara was on her way to class when Patricia hurtled toward her. "Something bad has happened to Joy, and the teachers are involved. I need your help."

"Uh-oh," Mara thought. She knew there was no point in trying to talk any sense into Patricia.

"I need Joy's home telephone number. I have to speak to her parents. All you have to do is act as a lookout while I steal her file from Mr. Sweet's office," explained Patricia.

"What?" cried Mara. "I'm not a good lookout. I always get caught first in hide-and-seek!"

Ignoring Mara's protests, Patricia sneaked into

Mr. Sweet's office only seconds before he walked around the corner. Mara stood there, panicked. "Say something, anything!" she thought. "Hedgehogs!" she blurted out.

"What?" said Mr. Sweet, raising his eyebrows.

"I'm genuinely worried about the plight of the indigenous hedgehog," Mara babbled.

Mr. Sweet was rooted to the spot by sheer disbelief. As Mara talked on about hedgehogs, Patricia dashed over to the filing cabinet and rifled through it.

"Come on, come on, quick, quick!" Mara thought. After what seemed like an eternity, Patricia found Joy's file and closed the cabinet door. She crept out of the office, right behind Mr. Sweet's back.

"Well, thanks for listening," said Mara. With a smile, she turned and walked away from a befuddled Mr. Sweet.

Patricia's mission had been a success . . . but she hadn't shut the filing cabinet door properly. Mr. Sweet noticed right away. He went through his files and discovered that the one for Joy was missing. Rushing to the phone, he dialed Victor's number. "We have a situation," Mr. Sweet told him.

Mara and Patricia returned to Anubis House triumphantly. But Victor had already swung into action. He was taking all the students' bags for inspection at the front door. "Something valuable has been stolen from campus. I am checking all bags so that I can eliminate you from my inquiries." He snatched Mara's and Patricia's bags. "Now get inside."

Mara and Patricia were horrified. "They know. Somehow they know!" whispered Patricia. The girls trudged into the living room, disheartened.

However, barely two minutes later, Victor waltzed in carrying everyone's schoolbags. "All bags checked and cleared," he said as he threw them in a heap on the floor. After Victor had left, Patricia pounced on her bag and looked inside.

"It's not here!" she said, holding her bag open. "He found Joy's file but didn't say anything. They don't want to get into any kind of discussion. It's easier to steal it back and say nothing. Now do you believe me about the conspiracy?"

"I have to say, I'm beginning to," admitted Mara.

7

That night, Nina opened the attic door and crept up the stairs, followed by Fabian. Nina stood next to the secret eye on the wall and touched it with her locket. The wall slid open. Fabian shone his flashlight into the utter darkness. A woman looked straight back at him. Fabian dropped his flashlight and stumbled back.

"It's okay," Nina said, laughing. "It's just a portrait."

She picked up the flashlight and inspected the painting more closely. It was the same girl as the one in the locket. As Nina passed the portrait to Fabian, she noticed three Egyptian hieroglyphics on the back.

"Curiouser and curiouser," she said. She turned to Fabian. "Quick, take a photo of the hieroglyphics with the camera in your phone."

After a long week of school, it was finally the weekend. Nina and Fabian decided to go back to the nursing home to see if Sarah had more information about the mysterious woman in the locket. When they got to the home, Nina knocked gently on Sarah's bedroom door. Fabian stood nervously near the entrance as Nina went in.

"I've come to ask you about the treasure. And also," Nina said, opening the locket, "who is in this picture?"

Sarah was about to reply when she noticed Fabian at the door. She gasped. "Don't let him take it, keep it hidden!" she cried. Nina tried to introduce Fabian, but Sarah grew frantic. "Hide it, quickly, hide it! Don't let him see!"

Nina hastily put the locket away as Fabian retreated. She stayed and talked soothingly to Sarah until the woman drifted off to sleep.

"The black bird, beware the black bird, there is danger," Sarah murmured.

Nina joined Fabian in the corridor of the nursing home and they walked home, trying to piece together what Sarah had told them.

"The girl in the portrait looks like you," Fabian said. "She has the same pretty eyes." They both blushed.

"Well," said Nina, "maybe a passing resemblance, but that's all. We still don't know anything about the girl in the picture, or the treasure."

"We do know the locket belongs to Sarah and it opens a secret panel in the house," said Fabian.

"Which means that Sarah, or Emily, or whatever her name is, must have lived in or visited Anubis House." Nina's eyes widened. "What if the girl in the painting is Sarah?"

"And what if the black bird is Corbiere?" said Fabian.

"Then we wouldn't have much to worry about, since it's stuffed," said Nina, laughing.

Dear Diary,

Curiouser and curiouser! I wanted to figure out the meaning of the hieroglyphics on the back of the portrait in the attic, so today I went to a rare bookstore and found a book called <u>Egyptology for Beginners</u>. Fabian and I looked through the book together and found out that the first symbol means "terraced hill," or "stairs," the second one means "hidden," and the last one means the number eight. Stairs. Hidden. Eight. I bet the treasure Sarah spoke of is hidden under the eighth stair! Maybe I've seen too much Indiana Jones, but Fabian and I are checking it out tonight!

8

Patricia spent the weekend investigating Joy's disappearance. While Nina and Fabian pored over *Egyptology for Beginners,* Patricia was talking to a policeman named Sergeant Roebuck. She had called Sergeant Roebuck earlier in the day and left a message, reporting Joy missing. Later that day, her phone rang.

"Patricia Williamson? This is Sergeant Roebuck. You filed a missing person report on one Joy Mercer?"

"Yes," said Patricia. "What's the news?"

"I'm happy to say I have spoken to her parents, and she is safe and well at home. I am sure she will be in contact soon."

"That's great news, thank you so much!" gushed Patricia. She hung up the phone feeling relieved.

"I've got an email from Joy," said Patricia happily a few hours later, as the Anubis House students readied themselves for dinner. "It says she's fine, but her dad's business went under and she had to leave school promptly. They couldn't afford the tuition anymore." Patricia frowned as she studied the email on her computer. "But there's no smiley face, and Joy never says 'promptly.'"

Everyone groaned.

"Give it up, Patricia," said Alfie.

"Enough is enough," moaned Jerome.

Even Mara couldn't take any more. "Patricia, how much proof do you need, for goodness' sake?"

Patricia thought long and hard.

"Sorry, guys, I guess I did carry it a bit far. Have I been driving you crazy?"

Everyone said a polite "No, it's okay" except Alfie, who said, "Too right you did, you nutter!"

Patricia turned to Nina. "And I owe you a special apology, Nina."

"It's nothing a few years of counseling won't fix. I'm just glad your friend is okay," said Nina.

Just then, Amber flounced in happily. Mick

had confronted her after she had kissed Alfie onstage, but they had talked things through and made up.

"Hi, everybody! Mick and I are back together, and we're having a party tomorrow night to celebrate," gushed Amber.

"Great," said Alfie, crestfallen. "A party. To celebrate Amber and Mick getting back together."

That night, the old grandfather clock in the downstairs hallway struck midnight as Victor dozed in his office. Nina and Fabian crept past him and tiptoed to the bottom of the stairs. They were ready to investigate the "eighth stair" clue they'd found on the back of the portrait.

"One, two, three, four, five, six, seven, eight," whispered Nina as she slowly ascended the stairs. Using a screwdriver, she pried the eighth step from its base and looked inside.

"There's nothing here." Nina sighed.

"Wait," said Fabian, looking a little closer. He reached inside the step and pulled out an old silver key. When he did, he knocked the screwdriver out of

Nina's hand, and it landed loudly at the bottom of the steps.

"Who's that?" grunted Victor, woken from his slumber.

Fabian and Nina fled down the stairs, but Nina wasn't fast enough. She pinned herself against the side of the staircase and prayed.

Victor came down the stairs, getting closer with every step. Closer and closer until . . . CRASH! He put his right foot straight through the eighth step.

"Aargh!" he cried, clutching his twisted ankle. He pulled his foot out gingerly and hopped up the stairs to his office.

Trudy came out of her room armed with a frying pan. She was looking for the source of all the noise but found only Victor trying to open the medicine chest. It was locked.

"What happened?" said Trudy.

"Isn't it obvious?" groaned Victor. He picked up his set of master keys and hopped over to the key cupboard to get the medicine chest key. He looked at the cupboard in disbelief.

"Trudy, do you have the spare attic key?" he demanded sternly.

"Of course not," she replied.

Victor's eyes darkened. "Well, somebody has it. Those students are up to no good, Trudy. Somebody is going to pay for this. You mark my words."

9

The next night, Mara sat on Patricia's bed, waiting for Patricia to get ready for Amber's party.

"I still don't trust Nina completely," Patricia said, finishing off her lipstick.

"Is it because she's American?" asked Mara.

Patricia frowned. "No, she's secretive. Just the other night, she sneaked something into a box under her bed. In fact, stand guard. I'm going to see what it is right now!"

Mara looked uncertain. "Well, okay."

Patricia dived under Nina's bed and scooped up a multicolored cardboard box. Opening it in a flash, she took a look inside. "Hmm, two keys. One is for the attic, but what's this one for?" she said as she held up the silver key from under the eighth stair. Then she spotted Nina's journal. "Oh, look! She's got a diary. Let's see what she has to say." Patricia set the key down and opened the journal.

Mara, leaning heavily against the door, was getting jumpy. "Put it back, put it back, please," she begged. "You can't read her diary!"

"Ha!" squealed Patricia, thumbing through the pages. "She thinks Fabian is geek chic."

Mara and Patricia giggled, but then Patricia's face clouded. "'But Patricia is possibly the meanest person I have ever met.'"

"See, I told you not to read it," said Mara.

"What a cow! And after I was so nice to her yesterday," said Patricia huffily.

The doorknob turned, and after a brief struggle, Mara was flung forward and Nina burst in. Quick as lightning, Patricia put the diary in the box and the box back under the bed before Nina could see.

"Party time," said Mara as they both scurried past a confused Nina.

The party was in full swing when Amber walked into the kitchen and saw Mara feeding Mick a tortilla chip.

"Very cozy," she thought.

Amber thrust a chocolate cake into Mick's hands. "Make an announcement," she demanded. "It's cake-cutting time."

Mick headed out of the kitchen, but when Mara tried to follow, Amber stopped her in her tracks.

"Keep your paws off my boyfriend," she said.

"What are you talking about?" asked Mara, blushing.

"I heard you tell Patricia that you fancied Mick, and you thought that he and I had nothing in common."

Mara was crestfallen. Earlier in the day she had indeed, under severe pressure from Patricia, admitted to liking Mick. Amber must have overheard.

"In a case like this, I think it's officially time to de-friend you."

"De-what me?" said Mara.

"De-friend you," said Amber. "And I am going to swap rooms. Patricia hates Nina, so she can have you instead."

Amber turned on her heel and walked out of the kitchen.

In the living room, music blasted over the sounds of students talking and laughing as they munched on snacks and danced. Nina pulled Fabian aside. "Now is the perfect time to go back to the attic. There's a party going on, so Victor is avoiding us. Do you want to come?"

Fabian grinned. "Let's do it."

Nina grabbed the attic key and the mysterious key from under her bed; then she and Fabian hurried to the attic. They searched and searched but found nothing. Just as they were about to give up, Nina noticed something. Hidden behind some larger boxes was a small wooden box with a keyhole. Nina's heart skipped a beat.

"Fabian," she cried, "this could be our next clue!"

They sat on a trunk and opened the box with the key they had found under the eighth step. Inside were some old metal cylinders and a jeweled case. They both stared blankly at the cylinders. Then Nina picked up the case.

"This looks really old," she said, holding it carefully. "I wonder what's inside?"

Just then, there was a loud crash nearby and

several boxes tumbled to the floor.

"We probably loosened them," said Nina, startled.

"Probably," said Fabian. "Let's get out of here. Grab the box and go!" With their newfound treasure, they dashed down the attic steps and rejoined the party below.

Dear Diary,

The mystery deepens! Fabian and I found a box in the attic that opened with the key from the eighth stair! We found some weird cylinders and a jeweled case that look really old. We almost got caught taking them back to my room, though—some huge boxes fell over and Victor must have heard. We raced back to the party without Victor seeing us, but then he came barging in and told everyone to stop the party. Everyone froze except Alfie, who was parading around wearing a deer head and shouting, "I'm a party animal!" He ran straight into Victor!

Victor grabbed Alfie, and everyone who doesn't live at Anubis House was booted out the door.

Victor told us that someone had been in the attic. He said that we might think he's stupid, but he's much cleverer than any of us. He then asked us for the attic key. Then Alfie started moaning, "My head's stuck. I can't breathe. I'm going to faint!" so Victor dragged him to his office to tug off the deer head.

Trudy saw what was going on and went to get some soap. I saw my chance to return the key, so I crept up the stairs toward Victor's office. While Victor was battling with Alfie's deer head, I put the spare key in the office, on the floor. As I made my escape, I just missed Trudy, who ran into the office shouting to Victor that she had soap and water. Trudy put the soap and the water bowl on the table and found the attic key, but Victor didn't believe that it had just dropped to the floor.

When I returned to the living room, I wanted to explain to the other members of Anubis House what had happened with the key, but Victor burst in and demanded to know which one of us had put it back. His eyes were wild when he asked each of us, "Was it you?" Finally, he got to me. "Was it you?" he yelled.

"No," I said. Then I thought a second and said, "Yes. I can't let everyone get in trouble for something I did."

You won't believe what happened after that!

Fabian came to my rescue. "No, she's covering up for me. I did it," he said.

Then Mick jumped in and said it was him! Then Alfie said it was him, and so did Jerome and Mara, and Amber said that she totally loves stealing keys! Even Patricia covered up for me and said it was her.

Victor grounded us all, but after he left, we all hugged and laughed. I'm beginning to feel more accepted here.

10

Before class the next day, Nina and Fabian decided to visit Fabian's uncle, who owned an antiques shop near the school. They hoped he would be able to identify the strange metal cylinders they had found in the attic.

"Ah, finally! Customers," said Aide Rutter as Nina and Fabian entered his shop.

"Not exactly, Uncle Aide," said Fabian. "It's me, Fabian, and I brought my friend Nina."

Uncle Aide smiled. "Finally, finally, you have a girlfriend!"

Nina and Fabian blushed. "No, no, just a friend, a good friend," Fabian blurted out.

Uncle Aide led Nina and Fabian to his back office, where he looked at the cylinders excitedly. "These play on an Edison phonograph. I don't have one, but I have a great book for you." He rummaged around and found a dusty old tome with a picture of an Edison phonograph on the front.

Fabian and Nina exchanged a glance. They had seen one in the attic!

"So," said Fabian, "there are recordings on the cylinders, like a tape."

"Yes," said Uncle Aide. "The cylinders are in good condition. The recordings should still be in tip-top shape."

Back on campus, Patricia had forgotten her French textbook and rushed back to Anubis House to grab it. As she reached the dining room, Patricia overheard Victor talking to someone. She recognized the voice but couldn't place it.

"Your phone call did the trick," said Victor.

The mystery voice asked if Victor was worried that the betrayer would return. Suddenly, Patricia realized that the voice belonged to Sergeant Roebuck, the police officer she had spoken to the other day! What Victor said next chilled her to the bone.

"We can take no risks. Anyway, it's over now. Joy is buried, end of story."

Patricia's head swam, and she thought she might faint. Instead she ran to her room. "Joy is buried, Joy is buried," she kept repeating to herself. "It can't be. No, it just can't be!"

Fabian was trying to close the front door of Anubis House while holding eight books about ancient Egypt. He lost his balance and fell, spilling the books everywhere. As he looked up, he gazed at the balustrade on the stairs from a new angle.

Fabian sprang to his feet. The repeating vertical pattern on the balustrade was the same shape as Nina's locket . . . and one of the symbols on the portrait in the attic. He had found a clue! He didn't know what it meant, but it felt important.

When Nina returned to Anubis House, Fabian excitedly pulled her aside. "I've been doing some research," he said. "The Frobisher-Smythes—the original owners of Anubis House—had a thing about Egypt."

He explained about the balustrade, and they agreed that the previous owners had written the hieroglyphics and hidden the cylinders in the attic. But why? The only way to find out would be to listen to the cylinders.

"Okay," said Nina, "the attic, at midnight."

"Agreed," said Fabian.

That night, Nina and Fabian sneaked back into the attic, opening the door with Nina's bobby pin. They placed a cylinder on the Edison phonograph and turned it on.

The old rusty machine released a terrible shriek that echoed through the house. Fabian and Nina desperately tried to stop the cylinder from rotating. Eventually, Nina pulled off the speaker and the cylinder ground to a halt.

"This is getting way too spooky," she said, clutching the speaker to her chest.

Dear Diary,
Tonight Fabian and I sneaked into the attic to

listen to the cylinders, but we had no luck. When I got back to my room, Amber was wide awake. She thought I had been on a secret date with Fabian! I decided to let Amber believe that Fabian and I were going out, and she promised not to tell anyone. I feel a little bad about deceiving her, but I'm not sure who I can trust.

· 11 ·

In drama class the next day, Patricia was staring out the window and thinking about Joy when suddenly, a man in a black coat appeared in the bushes. He looked straight at her. Patricia screamed.

"There's a man . . . in the bushes!" she cried. "Did anyone see him?"

Everyone crowded around the window. The man had vanished.

The bell sounded. As far as everyone else was concerned, Patricia was being paranoid. Classmates looked at her skeptically as they collected their books and backpacks.

"I saw him, I know I did," thought Patricia. Yet for the first time, she doubted her own sanity.

That night, Amber heard Nina as she slipped quietly out of the room. "Not this time, roomie," she thought as she pretended to be asleep. Earlier that day, she had spotted Nina trying to open a jeweled case, and she knew her roommate was up to something.

Amber waited two minutes and then got up. She checked her defenses. Garlic to ward off evil vampires—check. Tacky red shoes, carried, not worn, because they were high heels—check. She was set to go. She ducked out of the room just in time to see the attic door gently close. She approached the door and silently made her way upstairs.

As Amber entered the attic, Nina and Fabian were about to play the phonograph. They had oiled it so it wouldn't screech. They looked in amazement at her garlic and red shoes.

"What?" said Amber. "The Bible says 'Always be prepared . . . ,' or is that the Boy Scouts? Anyway, I'm prepared."

Nina sighed and explained to Amber what she and Fabian were doing. All three held their breath as Fabian slowly turned the handle on the phonograph. They heard the voice of a small child.

"Mother and father have given the house a name—

Anubis. They are going away soon to Egypt—for father's work. I'll be on my own again. With him. I am frightened. I don't want to stay here."

The little girl was softly crying as she spoke.

"I don't want to stay here either," said Amber. She was seriously spooked. As she stood up, she knocked over a table with a tray and pots on it.

"Amber!" said Fabian. "Quiet! Let's get out of here. Victor definitely heard that."

The three dashed down the stairs with Amber in the lead. As she stepped into the hallway, Victor rounded the corner. She quickly shut the attic door behind her. Nina and Fabian were on the other side of the door—trapped in the attic.

"What are you doing, creeping around after lights-out?" said Victor.

Amber looked like a deer caught in headlights. Suddenly, she struck a sleepwalker pose and walked straight toward Victor.

"Ice cream, brownies, yum, yum, food," she moaned.

"I was not born yesterday," said Victor.

"Well, I'm starving and I don't care about your

stupid rules. Fridge raid!" said Amber, and she bolted past a startled Victor.

"Amber Millington, you come back here!" yelled Victor as he chased her down the hall.

Dear Diary,

Amber's in on the mystery! She decided to follow Fabian and me into the attic and caught us just as we were about to listen to the cylinders. We had to tell her what we were doing. At first I was nervous because another person now knows about the mystery, but then Amber saved Fabian and me when Victor was about to discover us in the attic. She distracted Victor while Fabian and I unlocked the attic door with my bobby pin and ran to our rooms. She's full of surprises. Maybe she can be trusted after all!

12

In French class the next day, Amber showed Nina her state-of-the-art mp3 player. "Daddy bought it to help me study," giggled Amber. "But I thought we could use it to record those sphericals."

"Cylinders," Nina corrected her.

"Whatever. Anyway, that way we can listen to the recordings whenever we want."

Nina looked at her wide-eyed. "Amber, I will probably never say this again, but you are a genius."

That night in the attic, Fabian recorded one of the cylinders with Amber's mp3 player. Nina and Amber listened, saddened by the little girl's mournful voice.

"I wish my parents would come back. But I know they're not going to. I know it wasn't an accident. He did it. He murdered them!"

New girl Nina uncovers ancient
secrets hidden in Anubis House.

A mystery begins when an Anubis House
student, Joy, suddenly disappears.

Patricia is determined to find out what
happened to her best friend, Joy.

Fabian is your typical boy-next-door.
He has a secret crush on Nina.

Amber creates the Sibuna club to hunt for treasure in Anubis House. Nina, Fabian, and eventually Patricia and Alfie are members.

Alfie loves to joke around.

Victor is the creepy guardian of Anubis House. He spends
a lot of his time talking to Corbiere, his stuffed raven.

Working together, the Sibuna
club can find anything!

During their lunch hour at school the next day, Nina decided to go and see Sarah again. Fabian wanted to go too, but after the way Sarah had acted the last time, they decided he should stay put.

"Here, see if you can open this while I'm away," Nina said, handing the jeweled case to Fabian.

"We have to know if Sarah is the girl in the recordings," said Nina as Amber came skipping around the corner.

"You're going on a fact-finding mission without me? No way," said Amber. She grabbed Nina by the arm, determined to help out.

As the two girls headed for the exit, they bumped into Mick.

"Hi, Boo, good to see you. . . . Must dash," said Amber as she dragged Nina past him hurriedly.

"Remember our picnic at four o'clock!" Mick called to Amber as she and Nina disappeared down the hallway. Mick was confused. Normally Amber was all over him, but for the past couple of days, she had been ignoring him. "Oh, well," he said. "I'll get to spend time with her during our date this afternoon." Then he went to lunch.

"You said old, but I didn't know you meant, like, ancient," said Amber. She and Nina were at the nursing home, and Amber had just seen Sarah for the first time. "Has she never heard of moisturizer? It would take years off her."

"I think she is beyond caring about wrinkles," replied Nina.

Amber looked horrified that such a thing could ever happen.

Sarah was sleeping, but Nina gently coaxed her awake. "We found some cylinders and we heard a little girl's voice," she told Sarah.

"It's you, the one with the power," said Sarah.

"The little girl in the recordings, is that you, Sarah?" asked Nina.

"*The man who talks, he wants to stay forever; he wants to tip the Scales of Life,*" said Sarah dreamily. "*Sometimes I see their faces in the mirror, but I know they're not there.*"

"You are the girl in the recordings, aren't you? And your name really is Sarah," said Nina, grabbing the old woman's hand tightly.

"My mummy's dead, my mummy's dead,"

Sarah said over and over as she drifted back into unconsciousness. Nina and Amber weren't going to get any more information out of her that day.

After they returned from the nursing home, Amber and Nina summoned Fabian for a secret meeting. "Sibuna," said Amber, holding her right hand over her right eye in a sort of salute.

Nina and Fabian looked perplexed. Amber explained that since they were the only people in the house who knew of the mystery, they should form a club.

"'Sibuna' is 'Anubis' backward," said Amber.

"If this means we make a solemn oath not to tell anyone about this, then I'm in," said Nina.

"I guess I'm in too, then," said Fabian.

The three agreed to meet in the forest behind Anubis House to make their commitment to the club official.

A few hours later, Nina, Fabian, and Amber stood around a campfire in the woods. Behind them loomed a dark, lightning-struck oak.

Amber took the lead. "O ancient gods of Anubis House, we pledge ourselves to your secrets and your quest. We are the Sibuna club."

The three students agreed to protect the secrets of Anubis House and stand by their fellow Sibuna members.

Nina finished, "These are our sacred vows. Let no man or woman tear them asunder."

The heavens opened and it began to pour. Fabian turned to jog back to the house and tripped over a branch. As he stumbled, Nina saw the jeweled case from the attic tumble out of his backpack. She picked it up and began turning the sections of the case. As she manipulated it, she felt a strange force guiding her hands. Suddenly, the case split neatly into three pieces!

Each piece contained part of a riddle. When she put the pieces together, the riddle read:

**WHEN DAYTIME ENDS AT MIDDAY,
THROUGH TEARS OF GLASS
THE EYE SHALL SEE.**

The Sibuna members were in the living room trying to decipher their new riddle when Mick burst in. He stormed over to Amber.

Amber suddenly remembered that she was supposed to have had a picnic with Mick that afternoon. Her eyes widened. "Oh, Boo, I'm so sorry!" she said.

Mick wouldn't hear any of it. "That's it," he said. "We're done. And I hate it when you call me Boo!" Mick angrily turned on his heel and walked out.

Just like that, Mick and Amber were no longer an item.

Amber was devastated. She knew she had been neglecting Mick so she could help Nina and Fabian solve the mystery, but she hadn't realized it would end her relationship.

Despite her heartbreak, she decided to continue helping Nina and Fabian. The members of Sibuna agreed that their next move was to visit the attic and continue recording the content of the cylinders on Amber's mp3 player. As they listened to the mournful little girl's history, Amber lamented the loss of Mick as a boyfriend. "I love him, Nina, I really do!" she sniffled as Nina comforted her.

Then something caught Amber's eye. "What's that?" she asked, pointing to a stained-glass window in one of the attic walls.

Nina and Fabian sat openmouthed. "It's a picture of a sunset," said Fabian. "'When daytime ends' . . . sunset . . . 'at midday.' That's when it happens, at midday! Amber, you're brilliant!"

The same afternoon, Patricia was walking by herself through the woods outside the school. Out of nowhere, the sinister man she had seen through the classroom window appeared. He introduced himself as Rene Zeldman and placed a business card gently on the ground in front of her. She picked it up hesitantly.

"I am a private detective. I believe your friend Joy Mercer is in great danger. But I can find her with your help. Call me if you want to contact me. The number is on the card." And with that, the strange man was gone.

13

The next day in class, Patricia was telling Mara about the man in black. She pulled out Rene Zeldman's business card. "I saw the man in black again. He's real—and he's a private detective."

"Private detective," echoed Mara, not quite believing her ears. "Patricia, this really is getting out of hand." She might as well have saved her breath—Patricia was already dialing the number on the card.

Later that day, Patricia sneaked out to meet Rene Zeldman. The meeting got off to a bad start when he admitted having lied about his name.

"My real name is Rufus Zeno, and from now on I promise—total honesty."

Rufus showed Patricia a set of faded black-and-white photos.

"Do you recognize any of these?" he asked.

"Yes, I think. That," said Patricia, pointing to a symbol similar to the shape of the locket she had spotted around Nina's neck. "What is it?"

"It is the Eye of Horus," replied Rufus. "It may help us solve the mystery of Joy's disappearance."

Back at Anubis House, Fabian and Nina had been assigned baking duties to prepare for prospective students to visit that day. Fabian was trying to put some scones in an enormous two-door oven.

"Oh no," said Trudy as Fabian struggled to open the door on the right. "You'll have to use the other side. "That side has been stuck for as long as anyone can remember. Victor tried to fix it twice, but it just won't budge."

"Trudy, what was this place like before it became a school?" asked Nina.

"Oh, I guess it was much grander. The hallway definitely was. I've got some photos." Trudy rummaged through a bureau and passed a photo to Nina.

The photo was of a very large chandelier hanging in the foyer. "I think we have still that chandelier in the closet under the stairs," said Trudy. "Impractical but gorgeous."

Nina and Fabian looked at each other wide-eyed. In unison, and under their breath, they both said, "'Tears of glass!'" This was it. The next piece of the puzzle.

The puzzle had also mentioned a time—midday. Nina and Fabian would have to hurry to hang up the chandelier and solve the puzzle before noon.

Fabian persuaded Trudy that the chandelier belonged not in a storage closet but in its original place. Working quickly, Fabian and Nina refitted the chandelier in the foyer. It was nearly noon. Trudy was busy baking, and the coast was clear. Fabian dashed up to the attic to see if the stained-glass window of the sunset would yield the next clue.

"I hope this is the right 'tears of glass,'" thought Fabian as his watch ticked slowly toward twelve. Downstairs, Nina was having exactly the same thought as she stared at the chandelier.

The noonday sun began to appear through a window in the foyer. Suddenly, the light hitting the chandelier concentrated into shafts and beamed across the hallway. Before Nina had time to blink, a spot was marked out on the wall farthest away from her. Instinctively, she walked over and placed her locket on the spot.

The locket opened a secret compartment in the wall. Nina reached in and pulled out an exquisite jeweled cylinder.

"I don't know what this is for, but I'm taking it with me for sure," she thought. In the next instant, the shaft of light disappeared and the secret compartment slammed shut.

"After I finish helping Trudy with the baking, I need to call a meeting of Sibuna tonight in the attic."

That night, as Fabian, Nina, and Amber listened to the cylinder they had recorded on Amber's mp3 player, the voice of Sarah said something that chilled the Sibuna members.

"He frightens me. He is always stuffing animals in the cellar. But what frightens me the most is his raven, Corbiere."

In the background, they heard a voice.

"You have five minutes precisely, and then I want to hear a pin drop."

It was unmistakable. Unquestionable. The voice belonged to Victor. But it couldn't be. That would make Victor more than a hundred years old!

Later that night, Nina was walking out of the bathroom when the locket fell out of her pocket. Patricia pounced. Picking it up, she asked, "Where did you get this?"

"A friend gave it to me. Why do you ask?" replied Nina, snatching it from Patricia's grasp.

"Oh, no reason. It's just unusual, that's all," Patricia said, eyeing the locket.

Victor broke into the conversation by shouting, "It's ten o'clock. You have five minutes precisely, and then I want to hear a pin drop."

Patricia went straight to her room, grabbed her cell phone, and called Rufus. She told him what had just happened.

"Excellent," said Rufus. "See if you can grab it in the morning. I want to examine it."

As soon as Nina and Amber had left their bedroom the next morning, Patricia snuck in and rifled through Nina's clothing. Just as she was about to abandon the search, she found the locket in Nina's bathrobe pocket.

"It's always in the last place you look," she thought as she turned to leave—and walked straight into Amber.

"Why are you going through Nina's stuff?" asked Amber. "And what's that in your hand?"

Patricia tried to bolt for the door, but Amber stood in her way. She took the locket from Patricia.

Patricia panicked. "I wasn't stealing it!" she exclaimed. "Please don't tell Nina. There's a really good reason why I need to borrow it."

"Like what! A fashion emergency?" As Amber put the locket back in Nina's bathrobe pocket, she wondered whether she should tell Nina about Patricia's strange behavior.

Later that day, the Sibuna members were hanging out when Fabian managed to twist the top off their newfound clue. A crumpled piece of paper fell from the jeweled cylinder.

Fabian read it aloud. "'CET is the place to find. And there in the flames you must look behind.'"

"Even I don't know what that means," said Amber.

Fabian looked up "CET" in his Egyptian books.

"'CET' means 'place of fire.' If you reverse it, you get 'fireplace.' The only room with a working fireplace is the living room."

Nina and Amber ran downstairs. Amber tapped the fireplace. Nina tried to get behind it, but to no avail.

Just then, Victor came in. "First the chandelier, and now this. Something's going on around here, and I intend to find out what. Why are you fooling around with the fireplace?"

"Er, well, actually, we are c-collecting soot," stammered Nina. "For an art project about Pompeii. It's for extra credit."

Victor didn't believe her, but with no evidence to go on, he let the matter drop.

"I need to stay vigilant around this group of students," he thought, "especially since the Chosen Hour is nearly upon us."

14

It was dark and quiet outside Anubis House. Inside, students lay dreaming as silver moonlight played over their sleeping faces. Nina's clock said it was two a.m.

Down in the cellar, a sinister ritual was being performed. Victor, Mr. Sweet, Mrs. Andrews, Sergeant Roebuck, and three other shadowy figures were chanting.

"Ohnaa naa ohnaa . . . ohnaa naa ohnaa . . . ohnaa naa ohnaa." Everyone wore red gowns except Victor, who wore white.

Victor looked around at the many Egyptian artifacts in the cellar. A large statue of the jackal god Anubis had been placed prominently on his workbench.

"Brothers and sisters," he boomed. "The Chosen Hour fast approaches."

As he raised a giant hourglass, he spoke in Latin before welcoming an eighth member of the group.

The drama teacher, Jason Winkler, stepped from the shadows as the other members chanted around him.

The next morning, Amber was at the breakfast table when Patricia stormed in. She picked up a pitcher of water and poured it all over Amber.

"I asked you to keep a secret, and now you're siding with someone you've only known for two minutes!"

"Well, you went through Nina's stuff!" sputtered Amber. "That is sooo totally not cool. She's my roommate; of course I told her. And I would have told her anyway. Patricia, you are totally out of control. What's happened to you?"

"Some friend you are," said Patricia, and she stormed off.

She was on her way to school when Rufus stepped out of the shadows. "Did you get the Eye of Horus?" he asked.

"I nearly did, but it slipped away at the last minute," said Patricia.

"I need it," said Rufus. "And bring the girl it belongs to also. What is her name?"

Patricia frowned. "Nina Martin. She won't like showing her locket to a stranger."

"It doesn't matter. We must get to the bottom of what happened to Joy," Rufus replied.

After his meeting with Patricia, Rufus paid a visit to Sarah at the nursing home. He was talking gently and trying to coax information from her.

"Just relax. I only want to talk about the old days. Try to concentrate."

Sarah stared vacantly into space. Rufus sat back, frustrated. "I'll get you some tea," he said. "Maybe that will help."

Rufus left Sarah's bedroom just as the Sibuna members were about to enter. As the door opened, they ducked away to hide.

"Let's come back tomorrow," said Fabian, "when this guy has gone. He gives me the creeps. In any case, we need to see Sarah alone."

"Agreed," said Nina.

Keeping in mind that the latest clue had mentioned a place of fire, the Sibuna members decided to continue searching for the next clue. They went back to the living room and hunted everywhere. In the fireplace. Behind the fireplace and under the fireplace.

"I'm tapped out, literally," moaned Amber.

"Perhaps it's a different fireplace," said Fabian. "This place has central heating now, but there must be dozens of bricked-up fireplaces."

The Sibuna members decided to check the kitchen next. As they entered, Nina stared at the broken right-hand door on the oven.

"Could that be a 'place of fire'? We assumed the door was just stuck. But maybe it's something more than that." Nina walked over and placed her locket over the immense oven door that had refused to open a few days before. It swung open instantly. Secret steps led down to the cellar.

"Of course, I get it now," said Fabian. "CET . . . inferno . . . place of fire . . . hell. It means the depths of hell, a metaphor for the cellar. We've been looking in the wrong place!"

The Sibuna members crept down the steps into the cellar. It was dark and damp. And really spooky.

"Can we please put the lights on?" said Amber. "Bad things don't happen in the light, and this place is seriously creeping me out."

"Look," said Fabian, "we need to find a clue and get out of here." At that moment, he shone his flashlight on a metal ring attached to the wall. On the wall above it was a flame symbol.

"'There in the flames you must look behind.' It couldn't be simpler. That's it!" exclaimed Nina.

Fabian grabbed the ring, but in the damp cement it came away in his hand. He examined it closely. Etched on the inside of the ring was a set of numbers.

"Another puzzle piece!" exclaimed Nina.

Dear Diary,

Another close call! Fabian, Amber, and I were in the cellar and had just found the next clue when the lights came on! We dived for cover just before Victor came down the stairs. He opened a cupboard and took out a nearly empty vial, then went to a workbench and poured some of the vial's contents into a test tube. "Ah, so little left," he said, looking at the liquid inside. He raised the test tube high and said, "To life." Then he took a sip of the strange stuff and headed out of the cellar.

After Victor left, we came out of our hiding place and went to the workbench. Fabian picked up the test tube, but then Amber started freaking out and we had to leave. I wonder what Victor meant when he drank that liquid and said, "To life."

He's such a weird man.

15

Since Patricia couldn't take the locket to Rufus, she decided on another plan. "I have to get Nina to meet Rufus, for Joy's sake," she thought.

She confronted Nina later that day. "I'm sorry I was in your room, but I wasn't stealing your locket," she said. She made up a story and said she had a friend who was an antiques dealer. When she had mentioned Nina's locket, her friend had said it could be worth a lot of money.

"And this just came up in conversation?" said Nina, unconvinced.

"Yes!" replied Patricia. "That's why I was trying to borrow it. To show it to him and get confirmation of its value."

"It's funny, because where I come from, borrowing without permission is also called stealing," said Nina.

"Okay, I'm sorry! I was wrong to do that, but now I'm being straight with you," said Patricia.

Nina still didn't believe her, but she was intrigued by the possibility of finding out more about Sarah's locket.

"The locket isn't for sale. I'm holding it for a friend," she told Patricia. "But I will consider meeting your antiques dealer for an appraisal. Let me think about it."

Nina found Fabian and talked to him about Patricia's offer. Fabian said, "Look, I don't like it. It could be dangerous."

"It's someone Patricia knows. I don't think she wants me hurt. Then again . . ." Nina's voice trailed off.

"But it is someone who wants the locket."

"No," Nina corrected him, "someone who is interested in the locket. He may have information about its history and power." She paused. "I know! I won't even take it. I'll leave it with you. I trust you."

"Thank you," said Fabian, smiling.

Without her locket, Nina followed Patricia to meet the mysterious antiques dealer. As Patricia led

Nina down a path in the woods next to the road, Nina asked, "So what's the name of your friend?"

"Rufus," replied Patricia, and marched on.

"Why do we have to meet him all the way out here?" said Nina. She was getting nervous.

"Because we do," replied Patricia hurriedly. "Now, stop complaining. We're meeting him right here. Wait, no—get back!"

Through the bushes Patricia saw Victor putting a motionless body into the back of a van.

"It's Rufus!" Patricia exclaimed.

"But that's the man I saw at Sarah's yesterday," said Nina as she peered over Patricia's shoulder.

Nina realized that the mystery of Anubis House was more dangerous and complicated than she had thought. Since Patricia seemed to be in the thick of it as well, Nina decided to tell her about Sibuna in hopes that they would be able to compare notes. As she filled Patricia in on the details of the mystery, Patricia's eyes got wider and wider.

16

Later that day in class, Jason Winkler said he had decided that his students should write their own play. "Ideas, anyone?" he asked.

"I know," began Amber. "How about we write a story about a young girl who loses her parents in mysterious circumstances when they steal some treasure from an Egyptian pyramid. And then the girl is brought up by a weird guardian in a big old house. But then the guardian steals the treasure, and she gets help from some friends from the future. And the girls are then very rich. The end. Oh! Nina can help me write the script."

Nina and Fabian held their heads in their hands.

"That sounds promising!" said Jason. "Write up an outline in time for the next class."

Later that day, Fabian was in his room trying to decipher the numbers on the metal ring from the cellar when Nina entered carrying a laptop.

"You have to see this!" she told Fabian, opening the laptop.

Fabian looked at the screen. "This is about Howard Carter, who rediscovered Tutankhamen's tomb in 1922."

"Exactly," said Nina, and then she explained what she had discovered. There were twenty-three people in Carter's expedition party. Two of them, the Frobisher-Smythes, had lived at Anubis House. They had been accused of stealing items from Tutankhamen's tomb and smuggling them back to England. They had been tried and acquitted, but two jury members had been convinced of their guilt.

"To this day, the items have never been recovered," Nina breathed.

"So you're saying the treasure we're looking for could have come from Tutankhamen's tomb?" said Fabian.

"That's exactly what I'm saying," replied Nina.

Fabian's eyes gleamed. "Hang on a minute," he

said. He grabbed a piece of paper and constructed a matrix in which the numbers from the metal ring lined up in a few different ways. One way read 1922—the year Tutankhamen's tomb had been rediscovered!

"Can you imagine if there really are relics from Tutankhamen's tomb hidden in this house?" Fabian could hardly contain himself. "This could be huge. The next clue must somehow be linked to this date."

"It's 1922—the year Anubis House was built!" Nina cried. She also remembered seeing the number imprinted at the bottom of the Egyptian mummy casket that stood in the foyer of Anubis House.

They rushed over to the mummy. After fumbling for a few seconds, Nina touched the side of the plate with "1922" on it, and it opened to a secret compartment. She reached in and grabbed a small parchment.

As she stood up, the compartment closed with a thud.

**BEFEATHERED AND CLASPED,
HERE IS THE PLACE WHERE
YESTERDAY ALWAYS FOLLOWS TOMORROW.**

"I've got it!" said Nina, staring at the clue. "When we took the chandelier out from under the stairs, I saw a big box of leather-bound books in there. One could be a diary. That could follow the criteria of 'yesterday always follows tomorrow.' Sort of."

"Let's take a look," said Fabian excitedly.

They ran over to the closet and went through the books, which turned out to be photo albums. Nina picked up a photograph and shone her flashlight on it. She passed it to Fabian. "Look at this," she said. "It's dated 1925."

Fabian looked. It was a picture of a man leaning on a spade. He looked exactly like Victor! Fabian slumped down next to Nina. It looked like Victor hadn't aged a day since 1925!

Later, when Amber and Patricia found Nina and Fabian, they filled them in about the photograph.

"That is soooo creepy," said Amber.

"It gets creepier," replied Fabian. "There are three other ones taken years apart, and in all of them Victor looks exactly the same."

"Do you think he's a ghost, or do you think he's a vampire?" asked Amber.

"Neither, Amber, but I do think it's confirmation of"—Fabian hesitated—"a way to stop aging."

"Victor made a toast 'to life' when he drank that strange liquid in the basement," said Nina. "Maybe he found an Elixir of Life!"

Patricia was seriously spooked and wanted to hand the clues over to the authorities.

"We don't have enough evidence yet," said Fabian. "Photos can be doctored. We need to go back to the cellar and get a sample of the Elixir."

Just then, Jerome walked by and overheard the four talking. He stopped to listen.

"If it means going back into the cellar, then I'll go back and steal some of the stuff, and we'll get it analyzed. Don't worry, I'll go myself," said Fabian, looking at Amber.

But the girls wouldn't hear of Fabian going on his own. They decided to all go together.

"This calls for a practical joke!" Jerome thought. He ran to grab Alfie to help.

Patricia, Fabian, Nina, and Amber returned to the cellar. They were all extremely jumpy. The foursome went around searching for the test tube Victor had taken a drink from.

Suddenly, there was a thud.

"What was that?" said a terrified Patricia.

"Nothing," said an equally terrified Fabian. Just then, he found a test tube and pocketed it.

There was another bump, followed by a strange, mournful scream.

They turned their flashlights toward the source of the noises. A large wardrobe loomed before them.

Everybody froze in terror. The wardrobe doors flew open, and two creatures hurtled out. They had inhuman eyes, rotted teeth, and huge, bloodstained fangs. The students stood rooted to the ground.

One of the monsters lunged at Amber. Its huge claws grazed her face. She screamed and fled the cellar, with the others close behind.

17

At breakfast the next morning, the Sibuna foursome looked haggard. None of them had slept.

Jerome and Alfie sauntered into the breakfast area, high-fiving and laughing like maniacs.

"How did you sleep last night?" asked Jerome.

"Have you heard the rumors about what's hidden in the cellar?" said Alfie.

Amber looked terrified. Realization registered on the faces of the other three.

"I think we've found our zombies," groaned Fabian.

Jerome sneered. "I heard you guys talking about going into the cellar," he said. "And I thought, 'This is the chance for the prank of the century.' There's a grate covering the outside window on the far side of the cellar. Alfie and I managed to pry it open and jump down inside. And the rest, as they say, is history." Alfie and Jerome laughed as the Sibuna members fumed.

"Anyway, what were you doing in the cellar late at night?" Jerome asked with genuine interest.

Amber pretended to check her text messages. Nina and Fabian looked at their cereal bowls. Patricia looked at Jerome defiantly but said nothing.

"Ooh, haven't they gone quiet all of a sudden, Alfie," said Jerome. He didn't like being left out of anything. He decided at that moment to be more attentive to the movements of the other students in Anubis House.

After breakfast, Amber and Nina went to their room. Patricia and Fabian joined them.

"We still need to get the Elixir analyzed," said Fabian.

"For now let's just hide it. We'll decide later," said Patricia. She took the Elixir from Fabian and gently poured it into a plastic bottle. She snapped on the top and put the bottle in her bag.

"Look, I'm going to see Sarah this afternoon,"

said Nina. "I'll ask her about the Elixir."

"And Rufus, too," chimed in Patricia. "Ask her about Rufus. They obviously know each other. He went to see her that one time."

"Yes, and she might know why Victor has taken him," added Amber.

"Okay," said Nina. She was determined to get some answers from Sarah, even if he had to press a little harder than she liked.

Dear Diary,

Today I visited Sarah again. She seemed better than usual. I was so excited. I could finally get some answers! I asked Sarah if her mom and dad had ever talked about an Elixir of Life. Sarah said she didn't want to live forever, then changed the subject. She told me that she'd had a visitor the other day.

I asked Sarah if her visitor was Rufus. Sarah said yes and got a dreamy look in her eye. She told me they used to play together when they were children. That's so strange, because Rufus is so much younger than Sarah!

Sarah was starting to drift off, but I had to find

out one more thing. I took out the 1925 picture of Victor and asked Sarah if she knew him. Sarah freaked out. She started saying, "It's him! It's him!" over and over again. Then she said, "Child, he wants to tip the Scales of Life!"

I tried to calm Sarah, but she shrieked, "He's the one! He killed them! Now he wants to stay forever." She started rocking back and forth before she drifted to sleep.

Victor killed people! He actually killed people!

18

The drama students were practicing for the play that Amber and Nina had written. It was not going well. Nina had been walking a fine line while writing the script. She had wanted it to be realistic enough to shake up Victor but not so truthful as to endanger Sarah, or Sibuna, or anybody else, for that matter. As a result, the play was a hodgepodge of vaguely related scenes.

"We need girls in bikinis," Jerome suggested. "Just to liven things up a little."

"No, we need some more killing and lots of kissing," Alfie trumpeted.

"And we need more of the stuff that Sarah told us," Amber blurted out. Nina and Fabian shot daggers at her with their eyes.

"Who's Sarah?" said Jason.

Amber continued, oblivious that she was nearly giving away Sibuna's whole secret. "Basically, she's—" Fabian and Nina swung into action.

"A woman who works at the museum," finished Fabian.

"Yes, a research assistant, I think," said Nina.

Jason nodded. "Nina, why don't you go back and speak to Sarah . . . the research assistant."

Yet again, Amber's impulsiveness had nearly given away vital secrets. And now, with Victor a possible murderer, the stakes were much higher.

That afternoon, Alfie realized he had left his zombie mask in the cellar and asked Jerome to help him get it back. Jerome let Alfie into the cellar by opening the outside grate. Alfie climbed down through the window.

Victor appeared out of nowhere at the side of the house. "The cellar is off-limits!" he bellowed. "Get in the house."

Jerome fled and Victor shut the grate.

Alfie found his zombie mask on the cellar floor and went back to the grate, but it was wedged shut.

"Hey, Jerome," he cried. "This isn't funny. Let me out!"

But Jerome was gone.

Later that night, Fabian awoke from a deep sleep. "Oh, huh . . . what?" he mumbled. He opened his eyes to see Jerome peering at him.

"Alfie's trapped in the cellar. He's been down there hours. I'm not messing with you. I'm worried about him."

"Give me a minute," Fabian said sleepily.

Jerome and Fabian got Nina so she could use her locket to open the door in the oven to the secret passage. They searched the cellar, and then they heard a muffled cry coming from a nearby cupboard.

Nina opened the door. There, huddled and shivering, was Alfie. He was a mess, babbling insensibly with a wild look in his eyes. Jerome and Fabian picked him up and dragged him upstairs to bed.

19

The next morning, Jerome came running into the dining room, where the others were waiting for breakfast.

"It's Alfie," he said. Fabian, Patricia, and Nina raced to Alfie's room, and Mara followed.

Curled up in his bed, Alfie was twitching and sweating.

"You need to snap out of this," said Fabian.

"What did you see down there?" asked Nina.

"I saw . . . I saw . . . ," Alfie began, then started to hyperventilate. Patricia ran for a paper bag.

"He needs a drink," thought Nina. She grabbed a bottle from a nearby bag and handed it to Alfie. He took a sip, then began convulsing wildly and collapsed, unconscious. Nina looked at the bottle. She had taken it from Patricia's bag. It was the Elixir!

The students rushed to Trudy and told her about Alfie. Trudy called for an ambulance, and Alfie was taken away on a gurney, mumbling incoherently.

"I'll go with him to the hospital," said Trudy. "Had Alfie taken anything just before he collapsed?"

Nina hesitated, stepped forward, and hesitated again. "He took a sip of this." She handed Patricia's bottle to Trudy.

Trudy took a sniff. "Phew, smells awful," she said, and she followed the paramedics out the door.

As the Sibuna members gathered in Nina and Amber's room to talk about Alfie and the Elixir, Nina revealed that before she and Fabian had hidden the Elixir, she had kept a small amount of it in another bottle.

"I always like to have a backup plan," she stated.

Patricia grabbed the Elixir sample from Nina and promised to keep it safe. She went to the bathroom to hide it. As she was leaving, Jerome confronted her.

"What happened to Alfie?" he snarled.

"Grow up," said Patricia. "Hanging around the girls' bathroom is rather juvenile, even for you."

"Tell me what's going on down in the cellar, or I will go to Victor and tell him all about your secret passageway," hissed Jerome.

Patricia was not intimidated. "You'll do nothing of the sort. Because if you do, you will have to explain why you and Alfie were in the cellar in the first place. You're in it just as much as the rest of us."

And with that, she brushed past a defeated Jerome and stepped into the hallway.

While Patricia was hiding the Elixir, Nina told Fabian she thought everything was her fault. She felt like she was cursed. If she could turn back time, she would go back and not win the school scholarship.

Patricia and Amber walked in. "Well, Captain Nina," Patricia said, "Fabian hasn't solved the riddle, I can't get ahold of Rufus, and Alfie's still in the hospital."

"I can't do this anymore," said Nina tearfully. She took the locket from around her neck and gave it to Fabian. "Goodbye, Sibuna," she said, and left the room.

At breakfast the next day, Victor told the students that Alfie had drunk cleaning fluid. Nobody believed him.

Everyone wanted to visit Alfie, but Trudy decided that only two students could go. She chose Jerome and Patricia.

After Trudy left, Amber complained that Patricia would just yell at Alfie.

"I won't be yelling, I'll be interrogating," retorted Patricia.

"Don't try and confuse me with your made-up words," said Amber.

"I didn't make it up, dumbo," Patricia sneered. "It's in the dictionary!"

"It's in the dictionary," Nina mused aloud. Suddenly, she leapt to her feet. "It's in the dictionary!" she said, running over to the bookshelf. She grabbed a dictionary and began leafing through the pages until she found what she was looking for. Excited, she passed the book to Fabian.

"Of course!" he said, beaming. "The only place where yesterday always follows tomorrow. In a dictionary. You're a genius!"

Fabian picked up Nina and swung her around. Nina squealed with delight. When Fabian put her down, they avoided each other's eyes.

"Okay," said Nina. "That happened, but I'm still out, guys."

Fabian took the locket from his pocket and held it tenderly.

"Look, Nina," he said seriously. "Sarah gave this to you, not me."

Nina hesitated. She thought about how Sarah had trusted her to solve the mystery, and how her friends were counting on her. She looked at Fabian, Amber, and Patricia and gave them a big smile. "Okay, give it back," she said, and took the locket from Fabian. The others cheered. Nina was part of Sibuna again!

20

At the hospital, Patricia immediately demanded to know what Alfie had seen in the cellar. Alfie genuinely couldn't remember. He had completely blacked out.

Patricia turned to the nurse who was tending Alfie. "Did Alfie really drink cleaning fluid?" she asked.

"Well, he had an allergic reaction to something," said the nurse, "but we're still awaiting the toxicology results."

While Jerome and Alfie chatted, Patricia left the room and immediately noticed a man in a wheelchair in the hallway. He was slumped forward in a stupor. "I think I recognize that poor guy," she thought. "Could it be?"

It was Rufus.

With her heart pounding and limbs shaking, Patricia ran to the wheelchair. "Stay calm, stay calm," she thought as she released the lock on the wheelchair and wheeled Rufus out of the hospital.

Nina, Fabian, and Amber had been vainly searching for a befeathered and beclasped English dictionary that would point to the next clue, when Fabian had a stroke of brilliance and decided to look for an Arabic dictionary. They found one in the house with illustrated ornate feathers on the front and two heavy clasps locking it. Fabian broke a fork and a blade in his attempts to open the clasps, and Amber broke a nail file.

"Try the locket," said Nina, handing it to Amber. Amber tried using the locket on the first clasp, both gently and forcefully. She tried multiple angles. Nothing.

"Here, let me try," said Nina. She took the locket and placed it against the nearest clasp. Immediately, there was a glowing light, and the clasp sprang open. She moved on to the second clasp, which also opened.

"It only opens for you. Spooky," said Amber excitedly.

Nina opened the heavy book.

They saw a large hole, three inches by two inches, that had been cut from the front page almost through to the back cover. But the hole was empty. Whatever had been hidden there was long gone.

Fabian closed the book and the trio sat back, defeated. As they looked at one other gloomily, Nina received a text from Patricia. It read: I NEED HELP. MEET ME IN THE BIKE SHED.

Nina, Fabian, and Amber rushed out to the bike shed. They stood openmouthed when they got there. Patricia was putting a blanket over a mumbling Rufus. He was in a wheelchair and wore a hospital gown.

"You stole a patient!" gasped Nina.

"Have you gone completely insane?" said Fabian.

"Well, I couldn't leave him in the hospital—not like this, could I?" Patricia tucked the blanket around Rufus. "It's just until he comes around."

"And what if he doesn't come around?" said Nina.

"Of course he will," Patricia said calmly. "He's looking a lot better already."

As Rufus slowly came to his senses, Patricia explained that she had seen Victor kidnap him a few days before and that she had taken him from the hospital to keep him safe. "You thought Nina's locket might be the key." Patricia turned to Nina. "Nina, why don't you show it to him?"

Nina was flabbergasted by Patricia's betrayal and refused.

Rufus was very interested in the locket. He knew Nina had received it from Sarah and chastised her for taking it from a confused old woman.

"You must give it back to her. The locket is cursed. It belongs to Sarah Frobisher-Smythe—I can give it back to her if you'd like."

Nina jumped backward, and she and Fabian said in unison, "No!"

"Strictly speaking, the locket isn't yours," Rufus told Nina angrily.

"Strictly speaking, the locket isn't yours, either," replied an equally angry Fabian.

Rufus frowned. "The all-seeing Eye of Horus is evil. Even holding it poses a great danger."

"That's not true!" said Fabian. "The eye is a symbol of protection."

"Yes," replied Rufus, "but is it protecting good or evil?"

Exhausted, Rufus slipped back into unconsciousness. The Sibuna members decided to keep him in the shed for the night. They brought him more blankets and rushed back to Anubis House before Victor could catch them.

21

The next morning, Patricia stayed behind after breakfast to get food for Rufus. But when she opened the bike shed, Rufus had disappeared!

"I can't believe it!" Patricia cried. "He was my only connection to Joy." Nina and Fabian took the news badly too. They had pored over the Arabic dictionary and come up with nothing. Fabian had resorted to using a small flashlight to search every inch of the book.

"Wait, wait!" said Nina. "Shine the light over it again."

Fabian shone the light through the cut-out pages and onto the one remaining intact page at the back of the book. Something was happening. Slowly, almost imperceptibly, words began to appear.

"It's invisible ink!" cried Fabian. "The heat from

the flashlight must be making it appear."

The words faded in and out but eventually became permanent. The clue read:

**UNDER THE EYES OF HORUS
A GLOBE AND HOLLOW BE.
TWO RIGHTS FOR ETERNITY,
BUT JUST ONE LEFT TO DIE.**

"The panel in the attic is a kind of hollow. There's the Eye of Horus too," said Nina.

"True," said Fabian, "but that's not the only one. I think I know what this clue refers to."

Later that night, Nina and Fabian met at the bottom of the stairs.

"I've been thinking," said Fabian, "It says 'eyes,' plural, not 'eye,' singular."

"Eyes," said Nina.

"Yes," said Fabian. "The balustrade below the banister has multiple eyes! And look." He pointed.

At the top of the vertical columns on either side of the staircase were two ornamental orbs.

"Which one, though?" said Nina.

Fabian tapped first one, then the other. The second one was hollow.

"This one, for sure," he said.

"'Two rights for eternity, but just one left to die,'" said Nina. "That must mean if we turn it two times to the right, we get eternity, but if we turn it to the left, it must lock or something, and then the secret is left to die."

Slowly, carefully, Fabian turned the globe first once, then again. He pulled up, and the globe came off! Attached to it was a small, irregularly shaped gold object.

Fabian lifted it high. "What have we got here?" he whispered. It looked like an ancient puzzle piece.

Victor's voice boomed from above. "Yes, what have you got there?" He walked down the stairs, held out his hand, and said simply, "Give."

Fabian reluctantly handed over the strange object.

"I will decide upon your punishments tomorrow," said Victor. "Now get to bed."

Nina and Fabian hurried to the top of the stairs, but then turned, startled.

"What is this?" cried Victor, looking into the palm

of his hand. Realization hit him. "No! Nooo!" he cried. What he had confiscated was an Egyptian relic. He already possessed an object that was identical to the one inside the globe. He had believed he was in possession of an ancient Egyptian artifact called the one true relic. And now there were two!

22

The next day, the dress rehearsal for that evening's school play was about to begin. Pharaohs, English gentlemen, and fair maidens zipped this way and that. Amber, dressed as a cactus, was begging Jason to let her sing. Alfie had been released from the hospital and was feeling well enough to perform. He and Jerome looked comical in their camel suit.

Nina, Patricia, and Fabian were oblivious to it all. They were focused on the previous night.

"I heard him let out a cry. Victor sounded like a cross between a sick whale and a broken piano," said Nina.

"I saw him put the puzzle piece in his office safe," said Fabian.

"We have to get it back at all costs," said Nina.

"Even if we have to break into the safe and he knows it's us."

Victor found Mr. Sweet and Mrs. Andrews and told them about the new puzzle piece. Mr. Sweet grew weak and had to lean on his desk for support.

"We were so sure," said Mrs. Andrews, "that we were in possession of the one true relic, the Ankh. But we're not. Is that what you are saying?" She sat down heavily.

"No, we're not," said Victor. "There are more."

"Victor," said Mrs. Andrews. "The Chosen Hour approaches!"

Victor was well aware of the situation. The gloom deepened even more when he explained that he had received a phone call from the hospital. Rufus Zeno had escaped. Things were beginning to unravel all around them.

Dress rehearsal had gone well. Jason Winkler was pleased. Students high-fived and slapped each other on the back. Nina, Patricia, and Fabian jumped from the stage and huddled together. Nina was "Sally," a pseudonym for the real Sarah. Fabian was dressed as a 1920s English gentleman. He was playing the role of Howard Carter. Patricia was the god Anubis. With her plastic jackal head tilted upward and her real face pointed forward, she looked quite comical.

After the dress rehearsal, the three had several free hours before the performance, so they returned to Anubis House. Nina had thought of a plan to get the relic back from Victor's safe. She explained that during the school play, everyone would be in the auditorium. That would leave Anubis House empty.

"After the first two scenes, I'm not on again until the second act," explained Nina. "That gives me half an hour to sneak back, open Victor's safe, grab the puzzle piece, and be back in time for my second-act entrance."

"Brilliant!" said Fabian.

"Not brilliant," Patricia moaned. "Aren't you forgetting something?"

The other two looked at her blankly.

"The combination. We don't have the combination to Victor's safe."

Fabian closed his eyes. He mentally drew a grid, three by three inches, just like the safe's keypad lock. Miraculously, he remembered the placement of the buttons that Victor had punched the previous night to lock the safe. "He pressed the top right one twice, the middle one once, and the bottom left one once." Fabian opened his eyes and looked at the grid. "The code to Victor's safe is three, three, five, seven!" he exclaimed triumphantly.

Right before the performance of the play, Fabian's uncle Aide paid his nephew a visit. He had brought along a present, a book titled *Unlocking the Eye*. He had found it while rummaging through a dusty old corner of his antiques shop. "It might even be of some help to your Egyptian project," he told his nephew.

"Thanks, Uncle Aide!" Fabian said.

While waiting nervously for the school play to begin, Nina and Fabian looked through *Unlocking the Eye*.

"It's a story about Tutankhamen's secret lover, Amneris," said Fabian. He handed the book to Nina. "Here, read this," he said.

"'Before Tutankhamen's death, the god Anubis entrusted Amneris with the Cup of Ankh—the cup of immortality,'" Nina read aloud. She looked at a picture of someone drinking from the cup while surrounded by war. "'When the Elixir of Life is drunk from the Cup of Ankh, it grants immortality to all who sup from it. In the wrong hands, it could lead to tyranny, despots, and all-out war,'" she continued.

She turned the page slowly to reveal a picture of a girl in battle with the sun god, Ra. The girl was trying to protect the cup. "'Legend has it that Amneris buried the cup of Ankh with her lover inside Tutankhamen's tomb—where she hoped it would remain hidden forever.'"

Nina turned one more page. There was the girl with her hands across her mouth. The cup was gone, and a ray of sunlight marked the top of a pyramid beside her.

"'But there are some who believe that the cup was found and removed at the time of the tomb's excavation in 1922.'" Nina looked at Fabian. "So the treasure we're looking for is a cup that makes you live forever. No wonder Sarah is so desperate to keep it safe. And I'll bet that Victor knows about the cup and has been looking for it longer than we have!"

24

As the auditorium began to fill, Jason Winkler called all the players backstage.

Nina and Fabian peered through the curtain at the assembling crowd. Fabian spotted Victor sitting in the back row.

"What if it's a mistake to tell a thinly veiled version of Sarah's story in front of the man who ruined her life?" said Nina. She was genuinely afraid. Her mood worsened when she spied Rufus Zeno in row G.

"What's Rufus doing here?" said Nina. "This is getting out of hand!"

Backstage, Patricia, dressed as the jackal god Anubis, was in a panic. "I got a good-luck card this morning. It just says 'D4,'" she blurted out to Nina and Fabian.

"What does it mean?" asked Fabian.

"I was really hoping you would know," said Patricia.

"It could be a secret message from Rufus. He's in the audience," said Nina.

"What! Is he insane?" wailed Patricia. "What if Victor sees him?" She thought for a moment. "Maybe it's his seat number. Row D, seat 4."

"No, I just looked. Rufus is in row G," said Nina.

"Well, then who's in D4?" said Patricia.

There was no time to look. Jason came over and led Patricia to her place on the stage. "Curtain's up in thirty seconds," he said.

Patricia pulled on her jackal mask.

"Five . . . four . . . three . . . two . . . one!" counted Jason.

Patricia turned around to face the audience. At first the lights blinded her, but slowly she began to see more clearly.

The audience fidgeted as Patricia remained silent. She searched for row D, seat 4.

A small figure slowly began to take shape as Patricia's eyes got used to the lights. The person wore a hoodie that hid her face.

But Patricia knew instantly who it was.

"JOY!" she yelled.

Joy instantly froze. Patricia realized she had put her friend in danger. She began again, before Victor and Rufus could figure out that Joy was in the audience. "Joy . . . and sorrow. The joy of Egypt, the monarch Tutankhamen, is dead." Patricia then moved into the actual script. Joy breathed a sigh of relief and settled back into her chair.

At the end of the first act, Nina pulled off her costume and prepared to head to Anubis House to get the puzzle piece from Victor's office. "Good luck," said Fabian. "And hurry."

Nina smiled. "I will," she promised. She dashed to Anubis House and crept upstairs to Victor's office. She pulled a scrap of paper out of her bag. "I hope you got this right, Fabian," she thought as she punched in the numbers on the safe's keypad. She pulled on the handle on the safe, but nothing happened. The entry code was wrong!

Nina desperately searched Victor's office for the safe combination numbers. As she rifled through his desk, she noticed some coins tucked away in a drawer. Each coin had an Anubis House student's name engraved on it. "That's odd," she thought, before the sound of a slamming door below startled her. She dived under the desk to hide.

Victor entered the office. He had the money box from the play and was about to deposit it in the safe. As he punched the combination number into the safe, Nina managed to sneak her head out from under his desk and see the code.

Victor placed the money box in the safe and then took out the puzzle piece. To Nina's astonishment, Victor pulled out a second, identical piece.

"Why, why are there two, Corbiere? I thought there was only one. What if there are more?" Victor put the puzzle pieces back into the safe, locked it, and strode away.

Nina leapt across the office, punched in the new numbers, and pulled the handle. The safe swung open! She grabbed both puzzle pieces and bolted, knowing she was already going to be missed back at school.

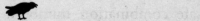

Nina burst backstage—and bumped straight into Jason. "You have three seconds to get onstage," he said.

As Nina pulled on her costume, Patricia and Fabian gathered around her.

"Did you get the puzzle piece?" asked Fabian.

Nina nodded before dashing onstage. She took a deep breath and began her lines. "My name is Sally, and I am seven years old. The truth has been heard, my story has been told. My parents' adventure has brought us only strife. The curse of Anubis has forever changed my life. . . ."

The rest of the play went off without a hitch. As the curtain fell, applause erupted from everyone in the audience, including Joy, who completely forgot herself and yelled out, "More!" Her hood fell back from her head.

Victor spotted Joy and ran toward her. She dashed out of the auditorium, but Victor trapped her, led her into a classroom, and locked the door.

"What were you thinking?" he barked. Just then, Patricia walked past the classroom shouting for Joy. Joy opened her mouth to yell.

Victor whispered into Joy's ear. "If you value

Patricia's safety, you must be quiet."

Joy looked at Victor. Her call for help died in her throat and she sat down heavily.

"Time to disappear again, Chosen One," sneered Victor.

Joy exploded. "I don't want to be the Chosen One, do you hear? I don't want it!"

"The choice is not yours," Victor said. Patricia's voice faded in the distance, and Joy shrank into her seat as Victor's shadow loomed over her.

Dear Diary,

Joy was in the audience tonight! Patricia searched for her after the play, but she had disappeared . . . again. At least we know she's still alive! Victor chased her out of the auditorium. I'm sure he knows what has happened to her. I don't know who is more evil—Victor or Rufus!

There are so many questions I have about the mystery surrounding Anubis House. What are the two puzzle pieces that I got from Victor's safe? Are they linked to the three other puzzle pieces—the bejeweled case in the attic, the jeweled cylinder in the foyer, and the metal ring in the basement—that we've found so far? Could the Cup of Ankh be hidden in the house? Is there really an Elixir of Life?

I have no doubt that Fabian, Amber, Patricia, and I will get to the bottom of this. Sibuna!